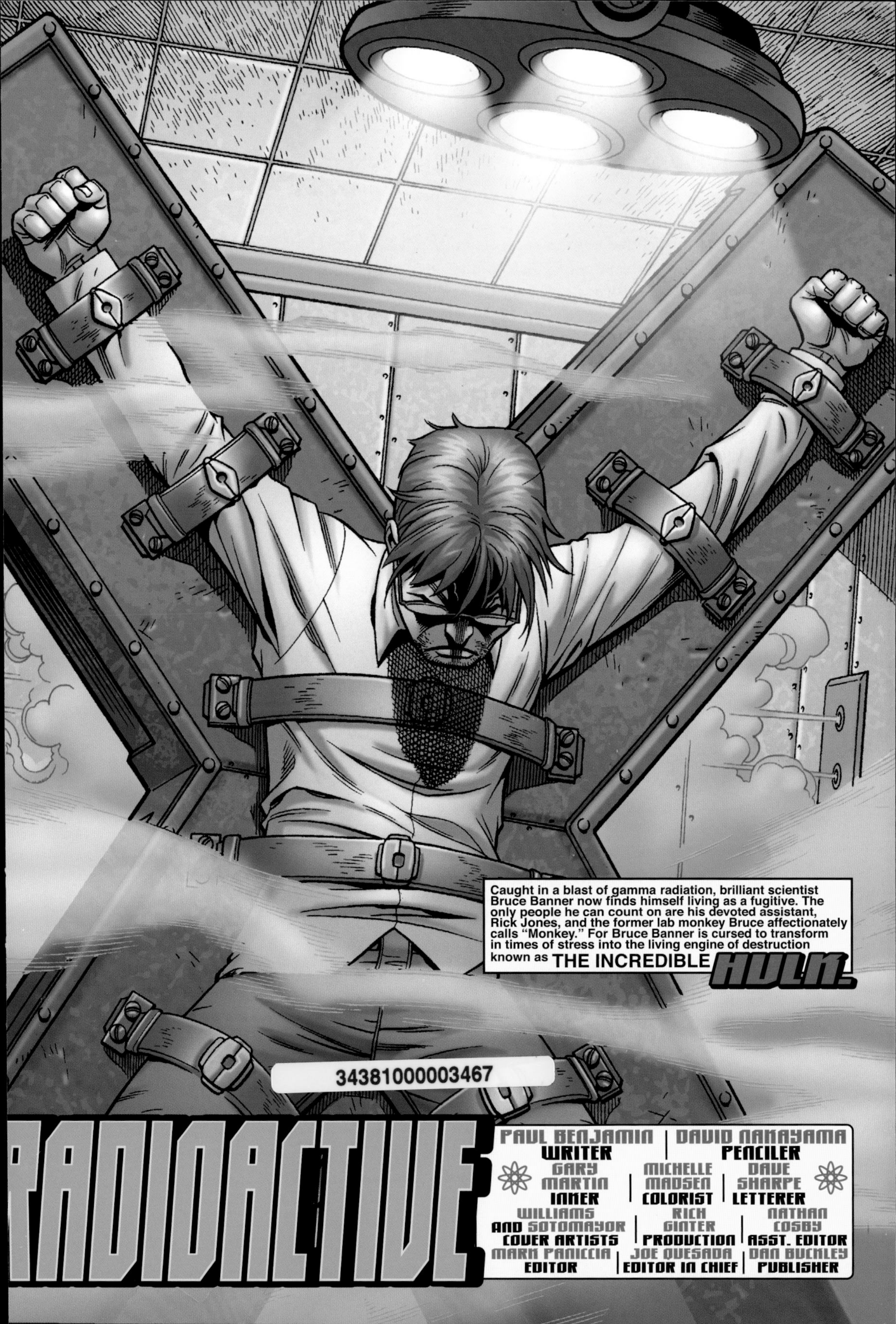

Caught in a blast of gamma radiation, brilliant scientist Bruce Banner now finds himself living as a fugitive. The only people he can count on are his devoted assistant, Rick Jones, and the former lab monkey Bruce affectionately calls "Monkey." For Bruce Banner is cursed to transform in times of stress into the living engine of destruction known as THE INCREDIBLE HULK.
RADIOACTIVE
PAUL BENJAMIN WRITER
DAVID NAKAYAMA PENCILER
GARY MARTIN INKER
MICHELLE MADSEN COLORIST
DAVE SHARPE LETTERER
WILLIAMS AND SOTOMAYOR COVER ARTISTS
RICH GINTER PRODUCTION
NATHAN COSBY ASST. EDITOR
MARK PANICCIA EDITOR
JOE QUESADA EDITOR IN CHIEF
DAN BUCKLEY PUBLISHER

Spotlight

MARVEL®

VISIT US AT
www.abdopublishing.com

Reinforced library bound edition published in 2009 by Spotlight, a division of the ABDO Publishing Group, 8000 West 78th Street, Edina, Minnesota 55439. Spotlight produces high-quality reinforced library bound editions for schools and libraries. Published by agreement with Marvel Characters, Inc.

Library of Congress Cataloging-in-Publication Data

Benjamin, Paul, 1970-
  Radioactive / Paul Benjamin, writer ; David Nakayama, penciler ; Gary Martin, inker ; Michelle Madsen, colorist ; Dave Sharpe, letterer. -- Reinforced library bound ed.
     p. cm. -- (Hulk)
  ISBN 978-1-59961-549-3
  1. Graphic novels. [1. Graphic novels.] I. Nakayama, David, ill. II. Title.
  PZ7.7.B45Rad 2008
  [E]--dc22
                                                            2008000103

All Spotlight books have reinforced library bindings and are manufactured in the United States of America.

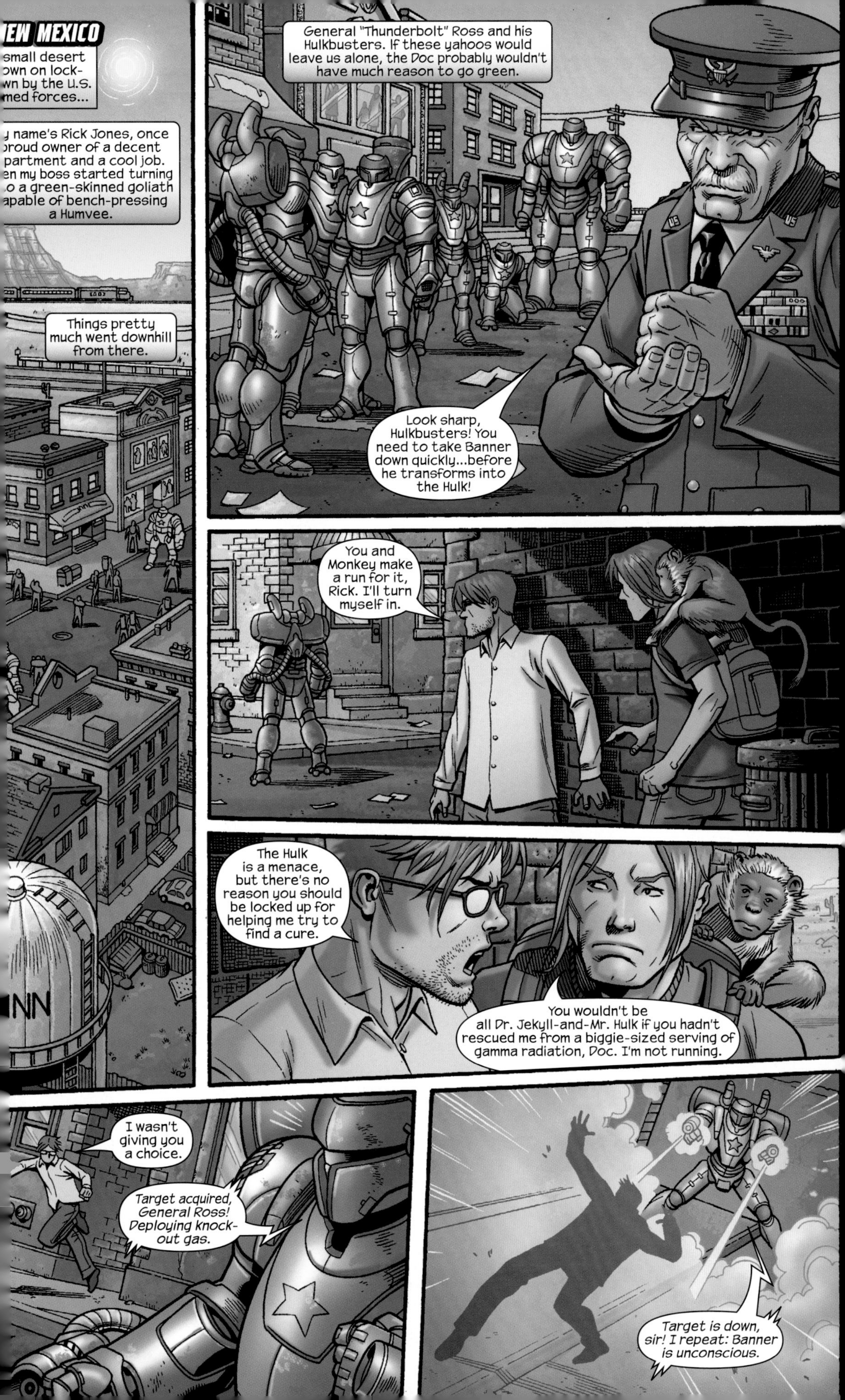

EW MEXICO
small desert own on lock- wn by the U.S. med forces...
y name's Rick Jones, once proud owner of a decent partment and a cool job. en my boss started turning o a green-skinned goliath apable of bench-pressing a Humvee.
Things pretty much went downhill from there.
General "Thunderbolt" Ross and his Hulkbusters. If these yahoos would leave us alone, the Doc probably wouldn't have much reason to go green.
Look sharp, Hulkbusters! You need to take Banner down quickly...before he transforms into the Hulk!
You and Monkey make a run for it, Rick. I'll turn myself in.
The Hulk is a menace, but there's no reason you should be locked up for helping me try to find a cure.
You wouldn't be all Dr. Jekyll-and-Mr. Hulk if you hadn't rescued me from a biggie-sized serving of gamma radiation, Doc. I'm not running.
I wasn't giving you a choice.
Target acquired, General Ross! Deploying knock-out gas.
Target is down, sir! I repeat: Banner is unconscious.

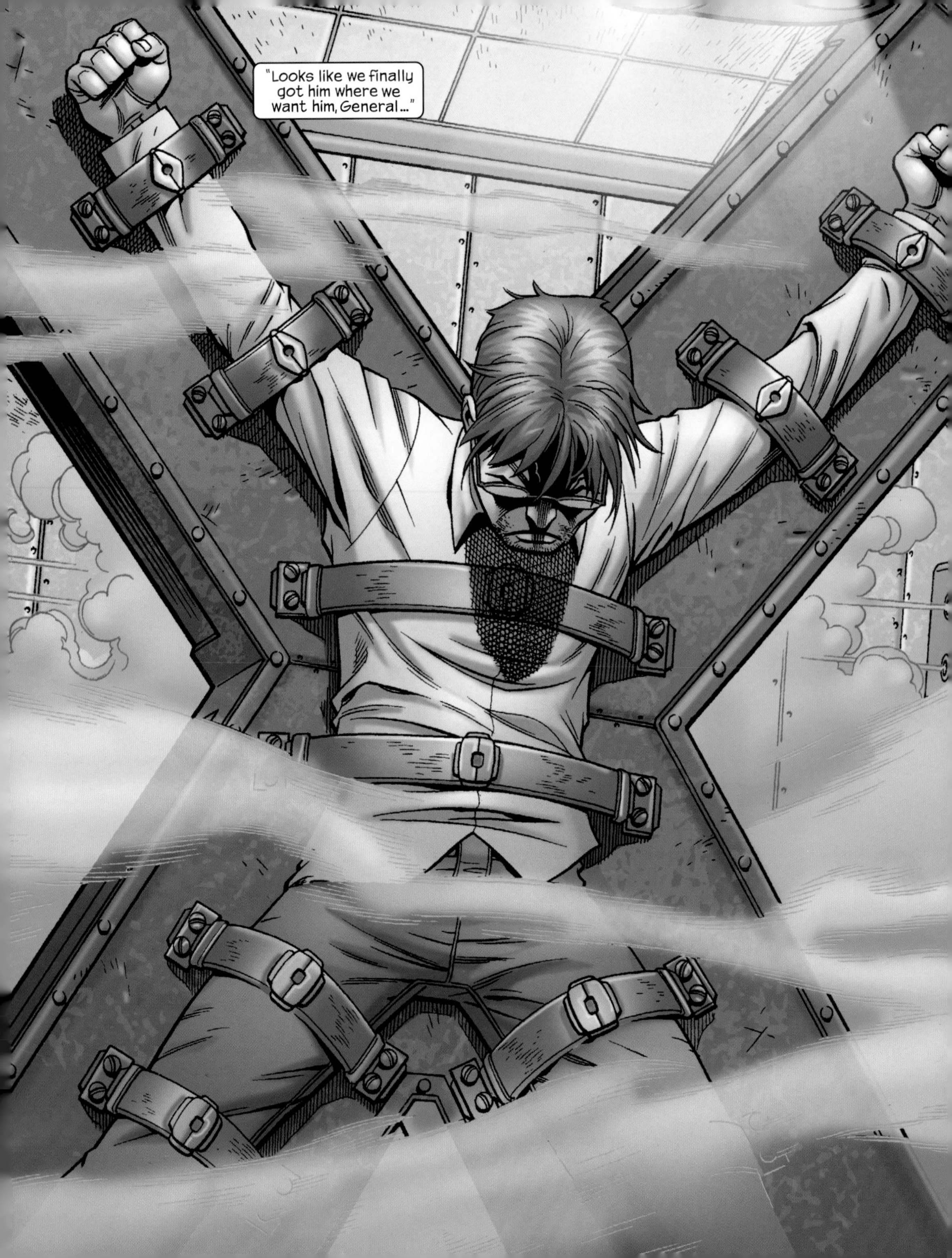
"Looks like we finally got him where we want him, General..."

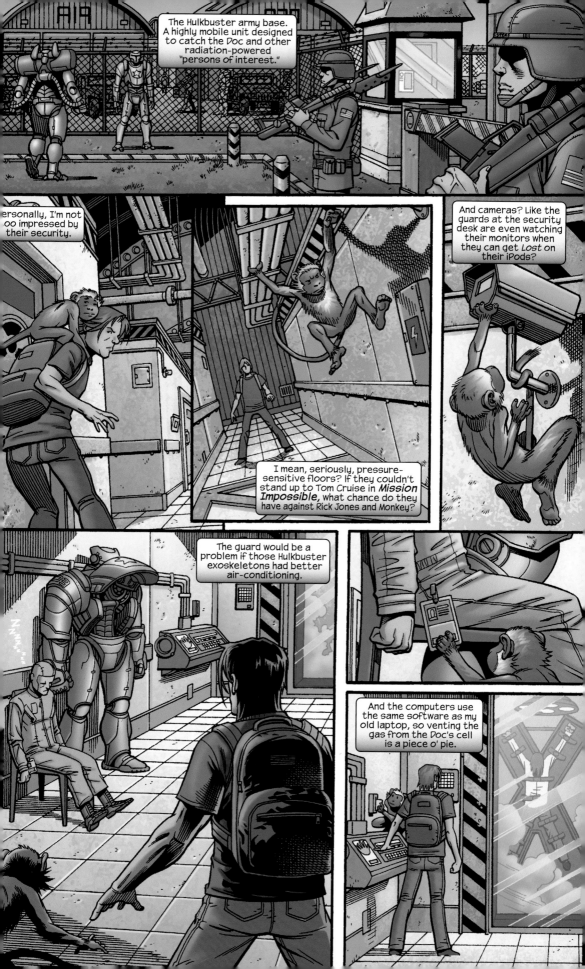

The Hulkbuster army base. A highly mobile unit designed to catch the *Doc* and other radiation-powered "persons of interest."

...ersonally, I'm not ...oo impressed by their security.

And cameras? Like the guards at the security desk are even watching their monitors when they can get *Lost* on their iPods?

I mean, seriously, pressure-sensitive floors? If they couldn't stand up to Tom Cruise in *Mission Impossible*, what chance do they have against Rick Jones and Monkey?

The guard would be a problem if those Hulkbuster exoskeletons had better air-conditioning.

And the computers use the same software as my old laptop, so venting the gas from the *Doc's* cell is a piece o' pie.

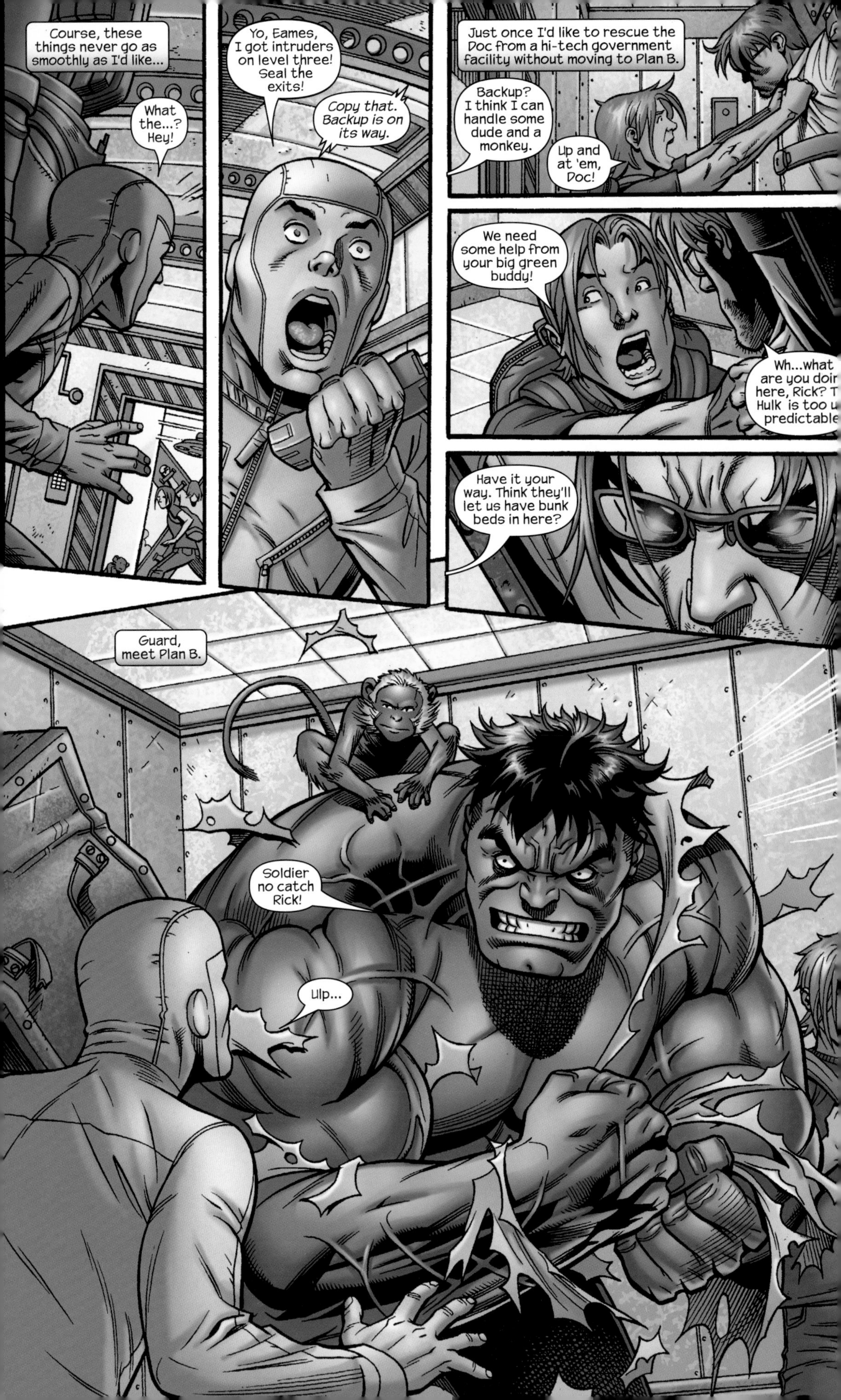
Course, these things never go as smoothly as I'd like...
What the...? Hey!
Yo, Eames, I got intruders on level three! Seal the exits!
Copy that. Backup is on its way.
Just once I'd like to rescue the Doc from a hi-tech government facility without moving to Plan B.
Backup? I think I can handle some dude and a monkey.
Up and at 'em, Doc!
We need some help from your big green buddy!
Wh...what are you doir here, Rick? T Hulk is too u predictable
Have it your way. Think they'll let us have bunk beds in here?
Guard, meet Plan B.
Soldier no catch Rick!
Ulp...

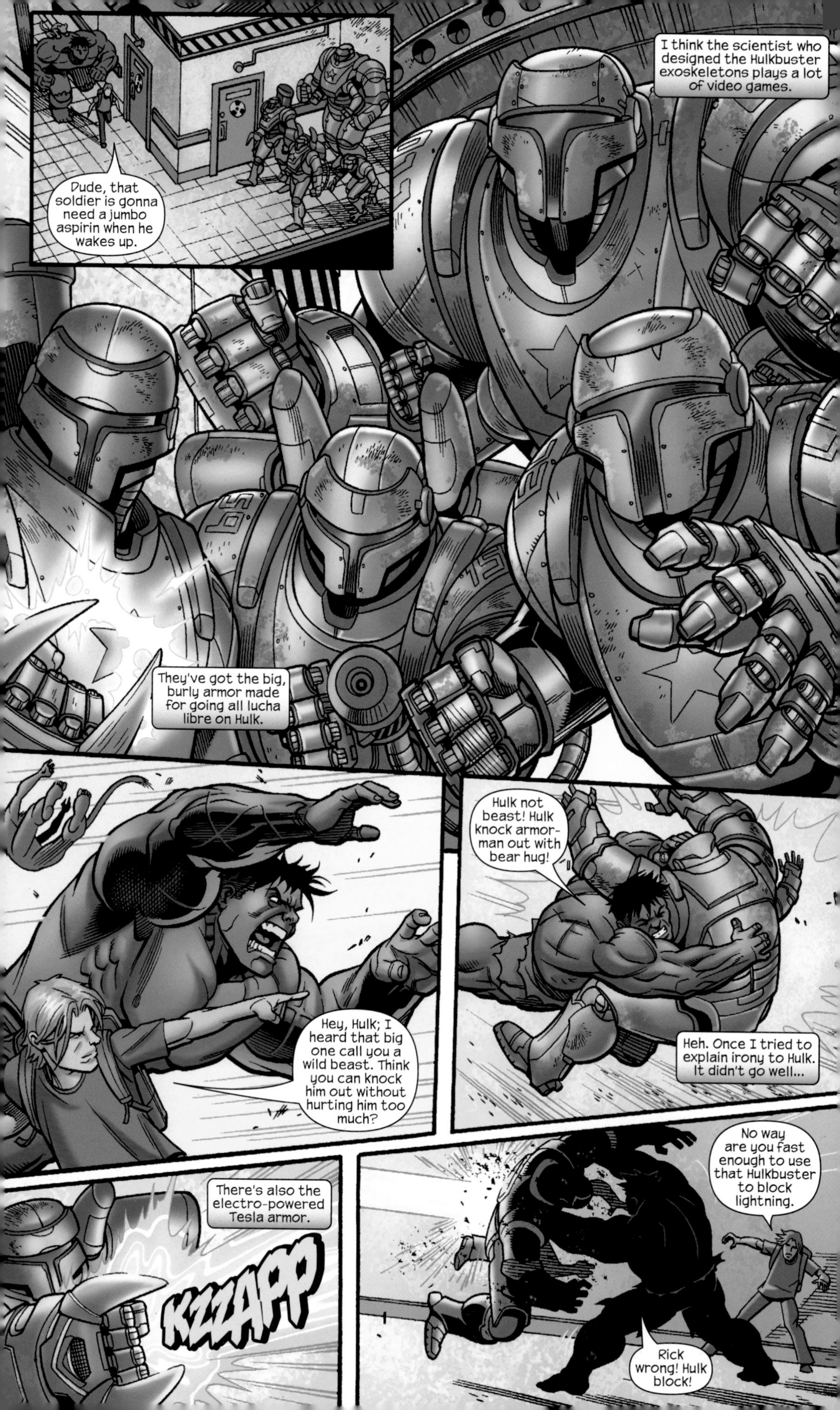
I think the scientist who designed the Hulkbuster exoskeletons plays a lot of video games.
Dude, that soldier is gonna need a jumbo aspirin when he wakes up.
They've got the big, burly armor made for going all lucha libre on Hulk.
Hey, Hulk; I heard that big one call you a wild beast. Think you can knock him out without hurting him too much?
Hulk not beast! Hulk knock armor-man out with bear hug!
Heh. Once I tried to explain irony to Hulk. It didn't go well...
There's also the electro-powered Tesla armor.
KZZAPP
No way are you fast enough to use that Hulkbuster to block lightning.
Rick wrong! Hulk block!

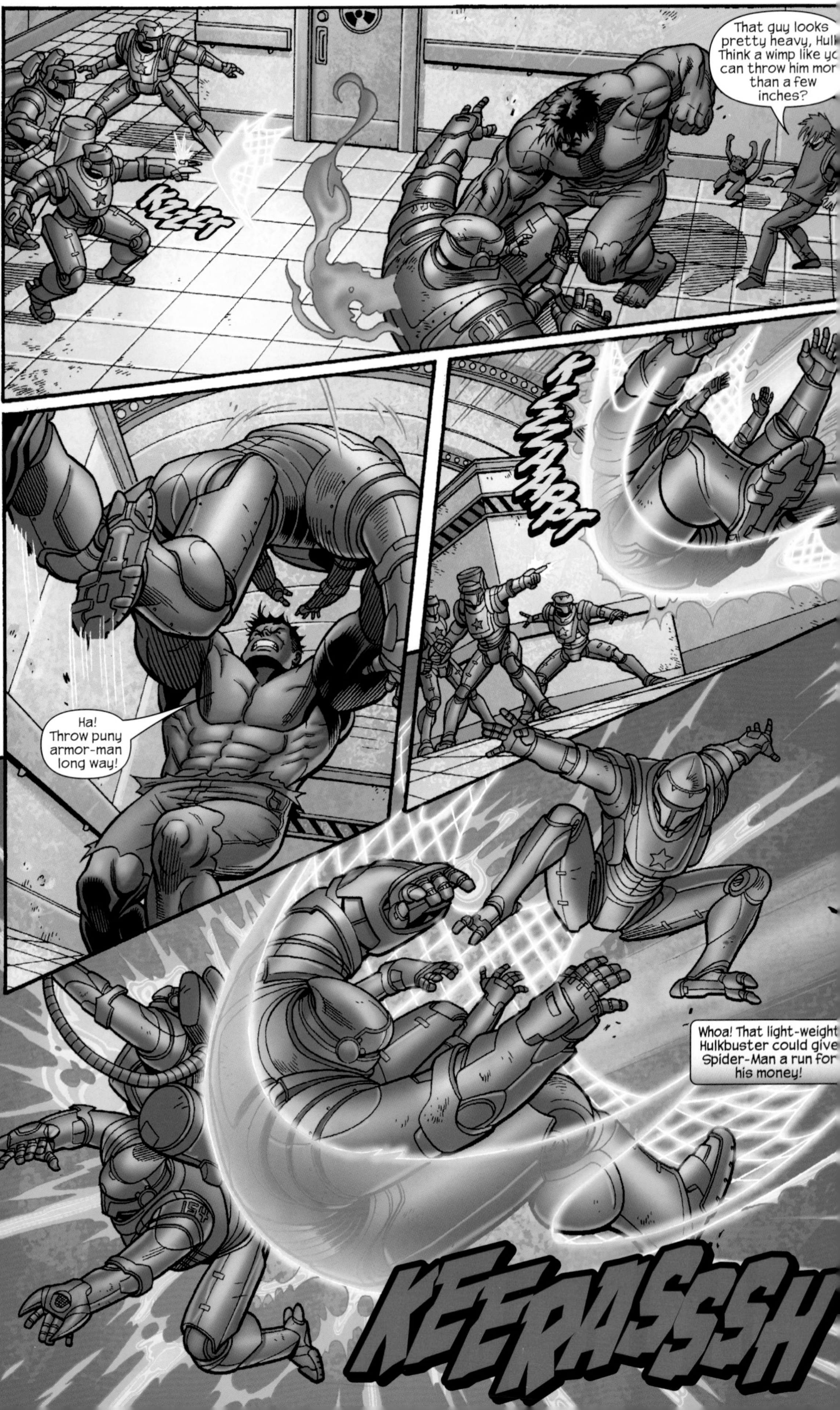
That guy looks pretty heavy, Hul Think a wimp like yo can throw him mor than a few inches?
Ha! Throw puny armor-man long way!
Whoa! That light-weight Hulkbuster could give Spider-Man a run for his money!
KEERASSSH

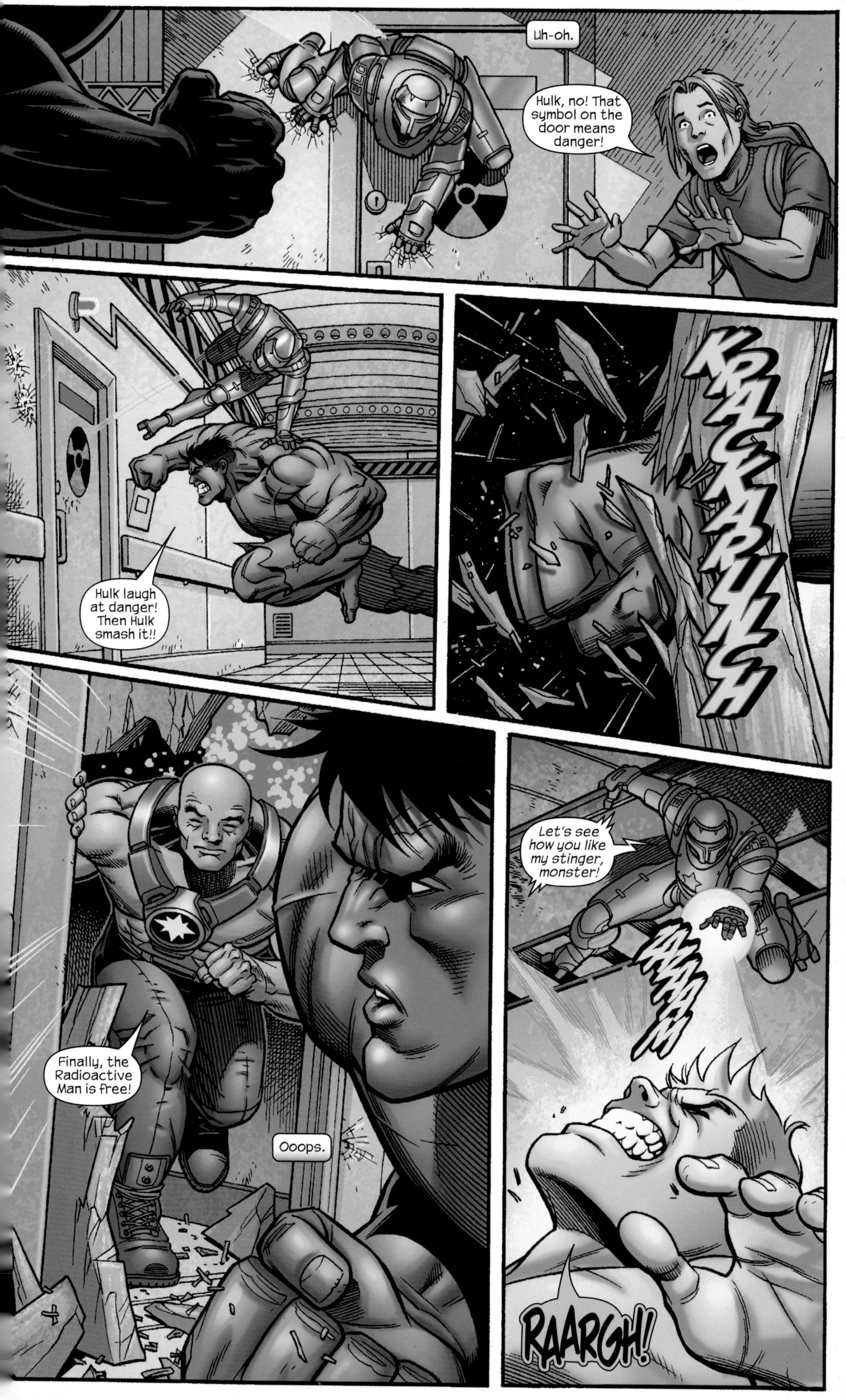
Uh-oh.
Hulk, no! That symbol on the door means danger!
Hulk laugh at danger! Then Hulk smash it!!
KRACKARUNCH
Finally, the Radioactive Man is free!
Ooops.
Let's see how you like my stinger, monster!
RAARGH!

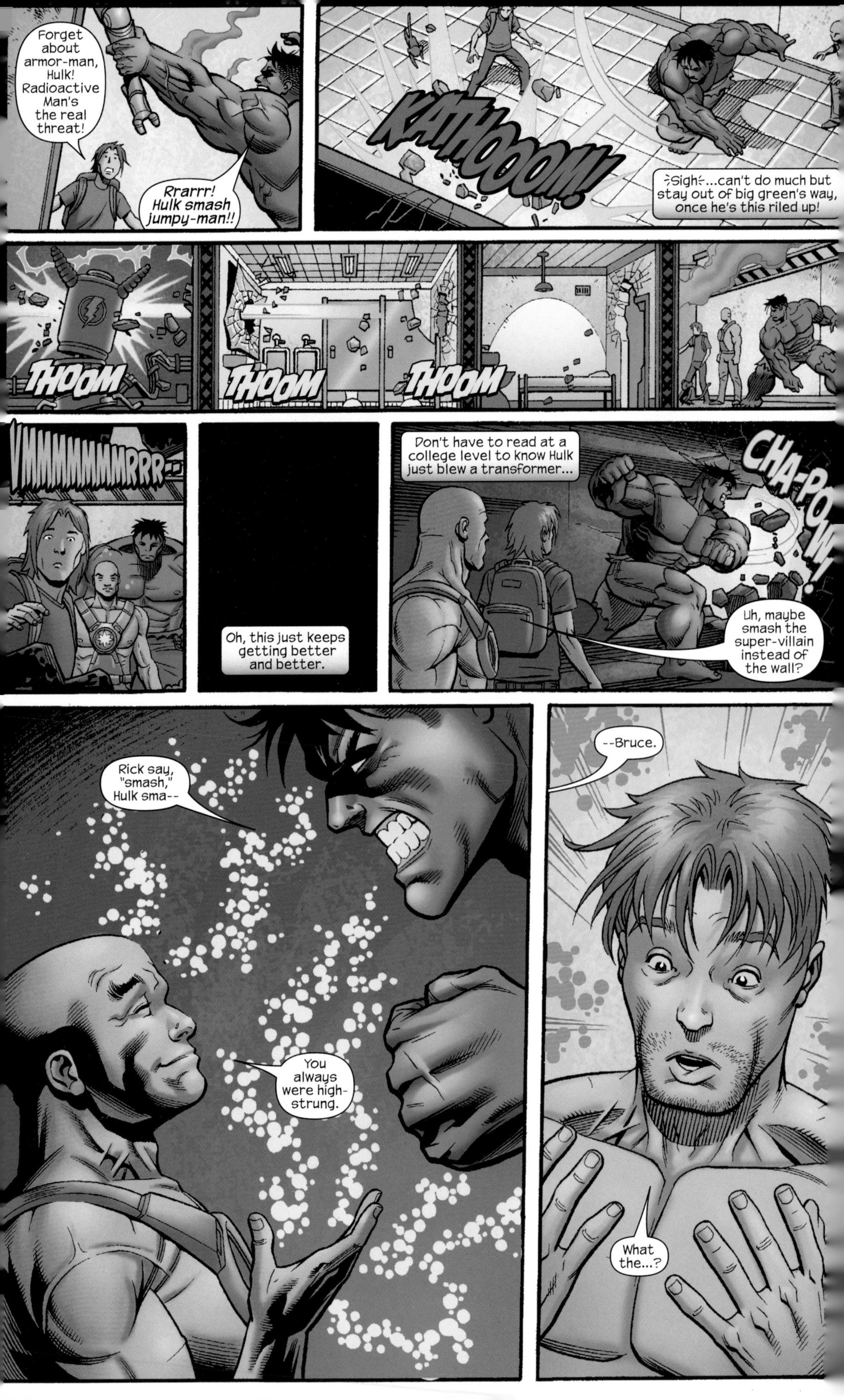
Forget about armor-man, Hulk! Radioactive Man's the real threat!
Rrarrr! Hulk smash jumpy-man!!
KATHOOOOM!!
~Sigh~...can't do much but stay out of big green's way, once he's this riled up!
THOOM
THOOM
THOOM
VMMMMMMMRRR
Oh, this just keeps getting better and better.
Don't have to read at a college level to know Hulk just blew a transformer...
CHA-POW!
Uh, maybe smash the super-villain instead of the wall?
Rick say, "smash," Hulk sma--
You always were high-strung.
--Bruce.
What the...?

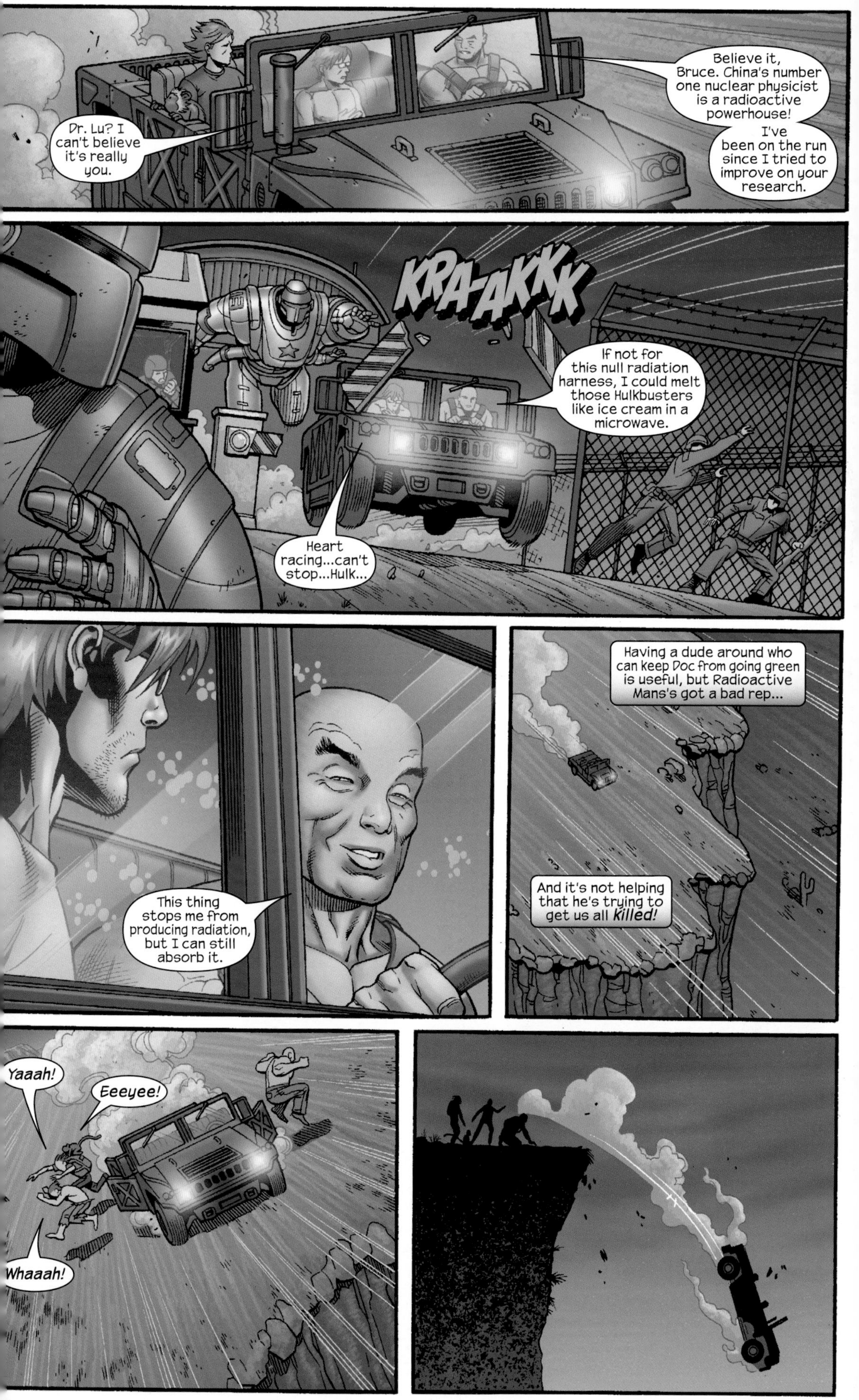
Dr. Lu? I can't believe it's really you.
Believe it, Bruce. China's number one nuclear physicist is a radioactive powerhouse!
I've been on the run since I tried to improve on your research.
KRA-AKKK
If not for this null radiation harness, I could melt those Hulkbusters like ice cream in a microwave.
Heart racing...can't stop...Hulk...
This thing stops me from producing radiation, but I can still absorb it.
Having a dude around who can keep Doc from going green is useful, but Radioactive Mans's got a bad rep...
And it's not helping that he's trying to get us all killed!
Yaaah!
Eeeyee!
Whaaah!

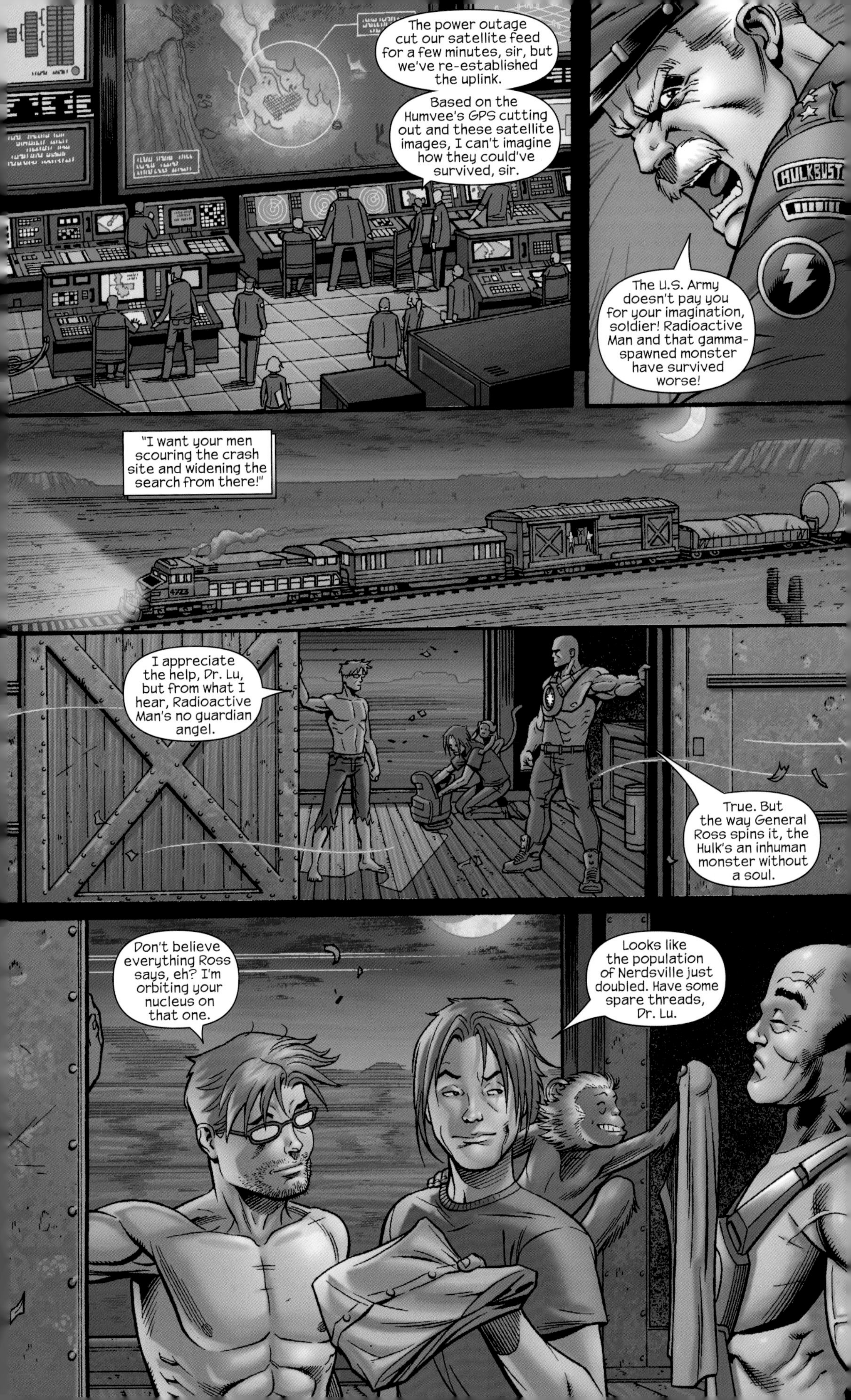
The power outage cut our satellite feed for a few minutes, sir, but we've re-established the uplink.
Based on the Humvee's GPS cutting out and these satellite images, I can't imagine how they could've survived, sir.
The U.S. Army doesn't pay you for your imagination, soldier! Radioactive Man and that gamma-spawned monster have survived worse!
"I want your men scouring the crash site and widening the search from there!"
I appreciate the help, Dr. Lu, but from what I hear, Radioactive Man's no guardian angel.
True. But the way General Ross spins it, the Hulk's an inhuman monster without a soul.
Don't believe everything Ross says, eh? I'm orbiting your nucleus on that one.
Looks like the population of Nerdsville just doubled. Have some spare threads, Dr. Lu.

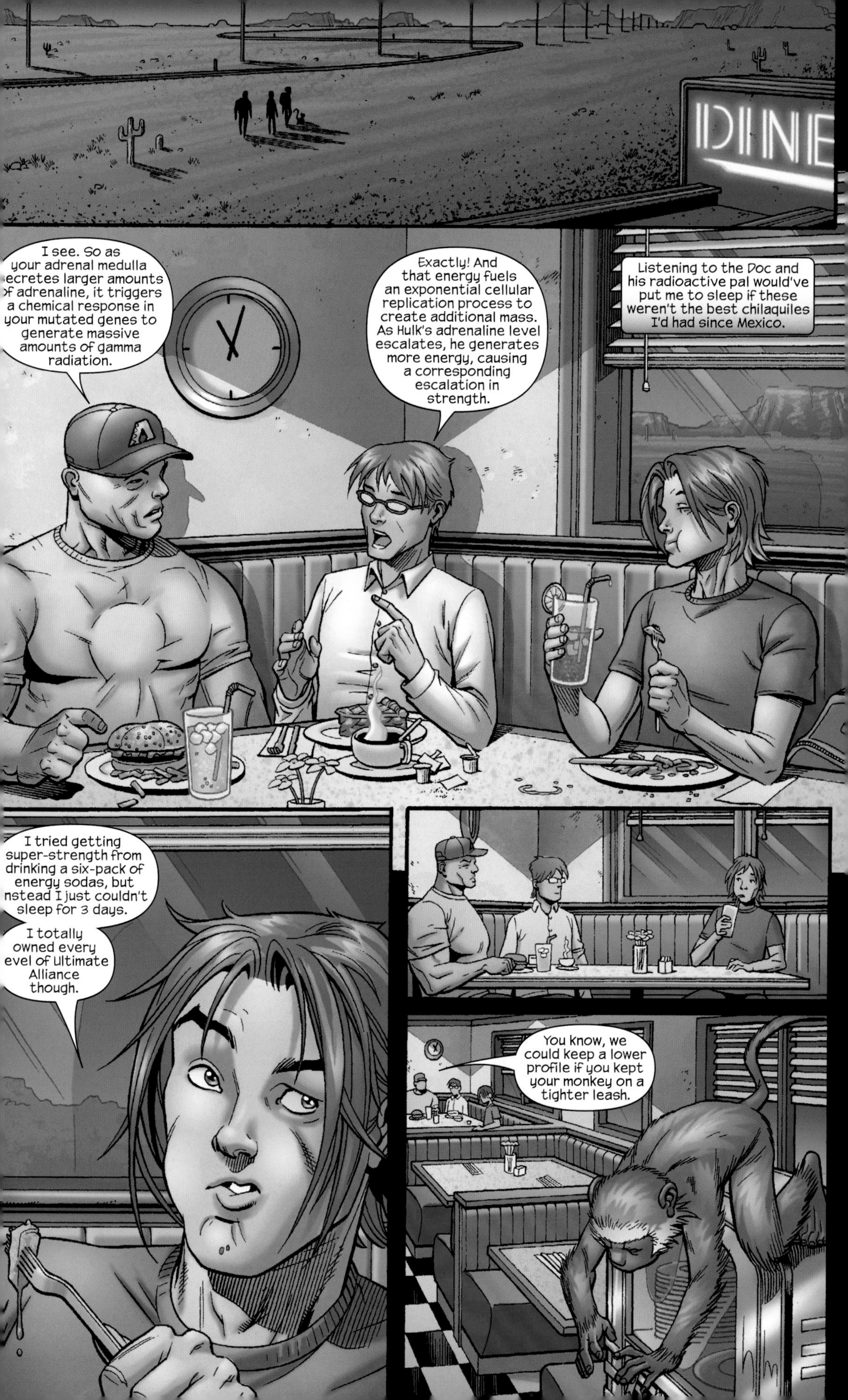
DINE
I see. So as your adrenal medulla secretes larger amounts of adrenaline, it triggers a chemical response in your mutated genes to generate massive amounts of gamma radiation.
Exactly! And that energy fuels an exponential cellular replication process to create additional mass. As Hulk's adrenaline level escalates, he generates more energy, causing a corresponding escalation in strength.
Listening to the Doc and his radioactive pal would've put me to sleep if these weren't the best chilaquiles I'd had since Mexico.
I tried getting super-strength from drinking a six-pack of energy sodas, but instead I just couldn't sleep for 3 days.
I totally owned every level of Ultimate Alliance though.
You know, we could keep a lower profile if you kept your monkey on a tighter leash.

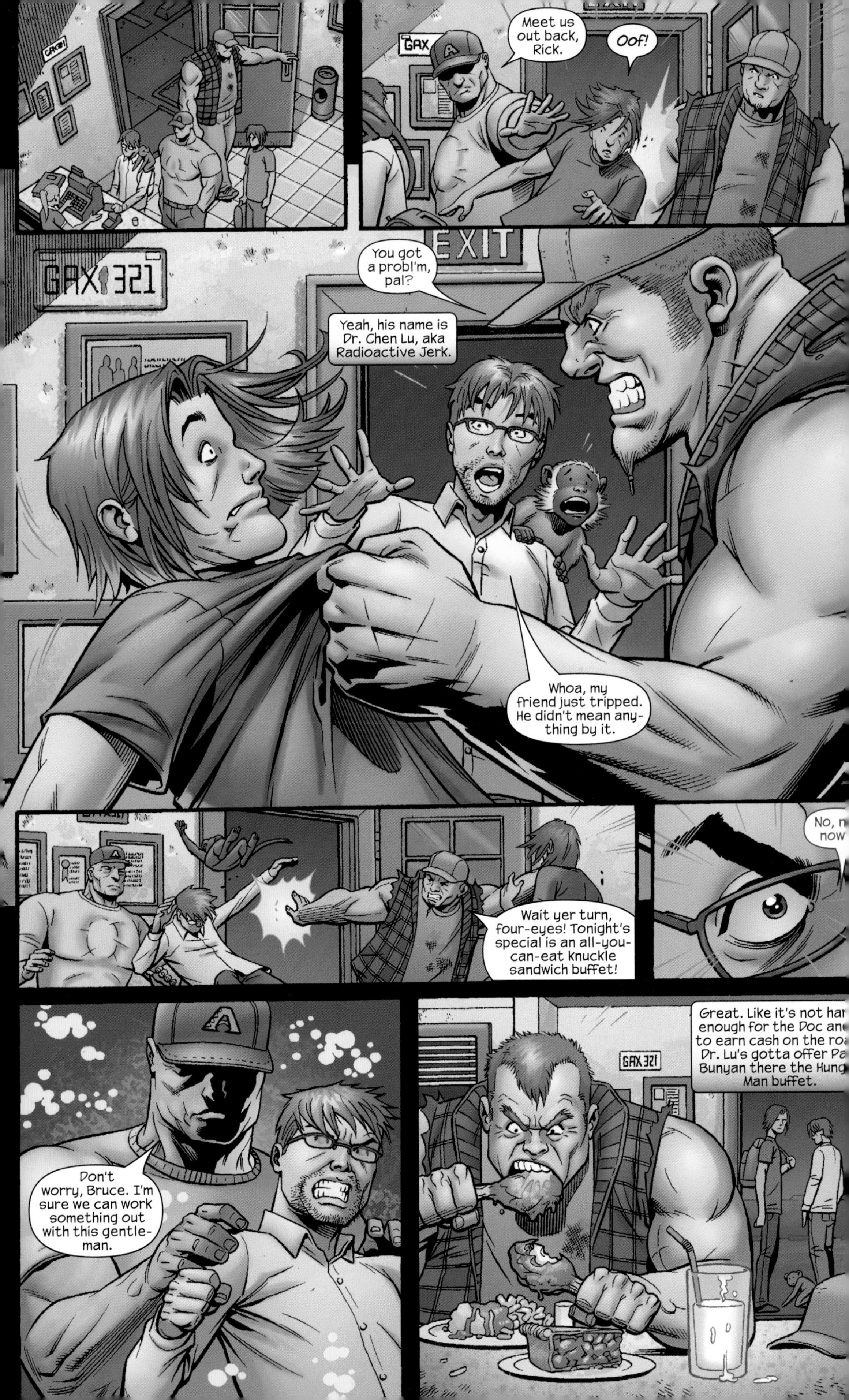
Meet us out back, Rick.
Oof!
GAX 321
EXIT
You got a probl'm, pal?
Yeah, his name is Dr. Chen Lu, aka Radioactive Jerk.
Whoa, my friend just tripped. He didn't mean anything by it.
Wait yer turn, four-eyes! Tonight's special is an all-you-can-eat knuckle sandwich buffet!
No, n now
Don't worry, Bruce. I'm sure we can work something out with this gentleman.
GAX 321
Great. Like it's not har enough for the Doc an to earn cash on the ro Dr. Lu's gotta offer Pa Bunyan there the Hung Man buffet.

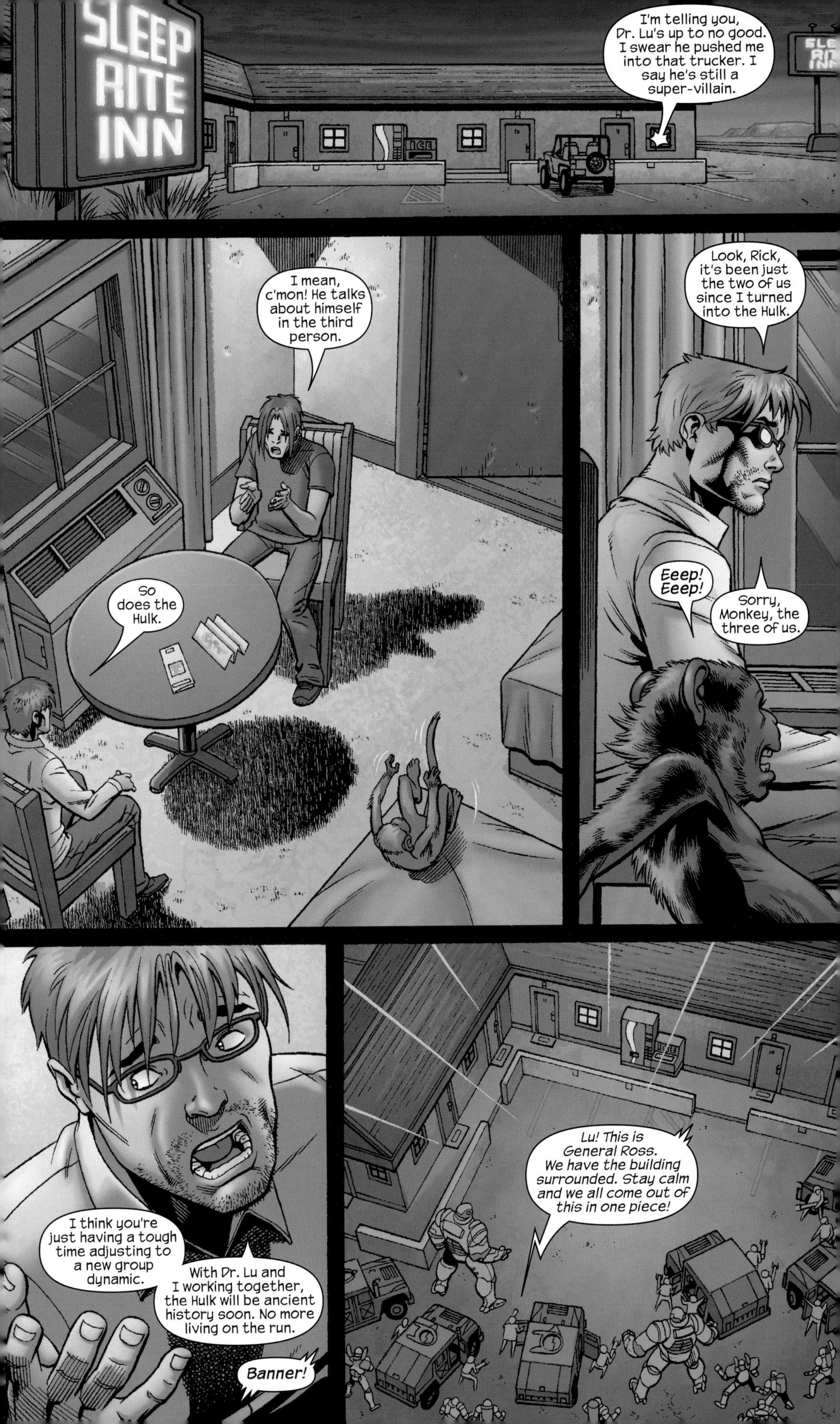
SLEEP RITE INN
I'm telling you, Dr. Lu's up to no good. I swear he pushed me into that trucker. I say he's still a super-villain.
ICE
I mean, c'mon! He talks about himself in the third person.
So does the Hulk.
Look, Rick, it's been just the two of us since I turned into the Hulk.
Eeep! Eeep!
Sorry, Monkey, the three of us.
I think you're just having a tough time adjusting to a new group dynamic.
With Dr. Lu and I working together, the Hulk will be ancient history soon. No more living on the run.
Banner!
Lu! This is General Ross. We have the building surrounded. Stay calm and we all come out of this in one piece!

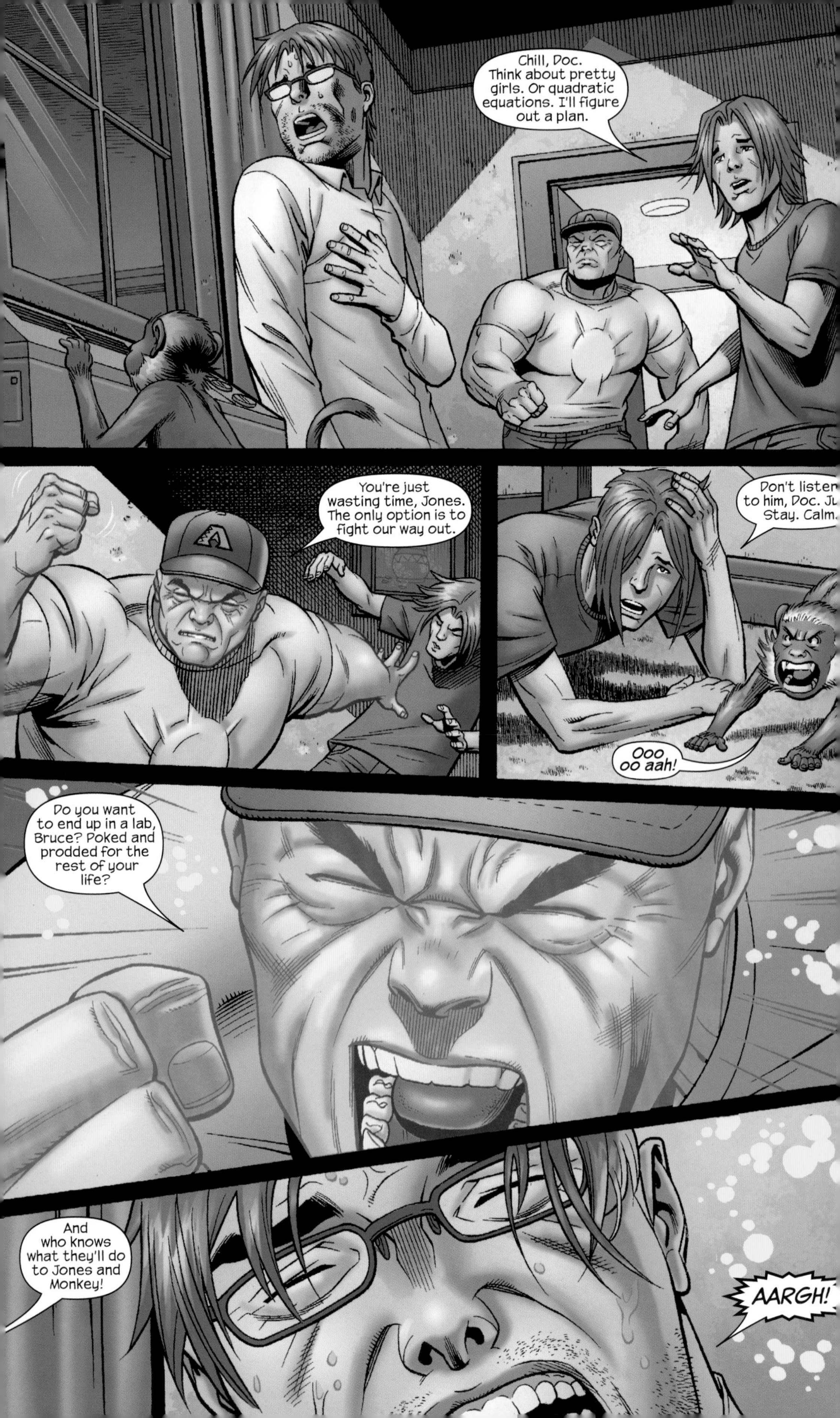
Chill, Doc. Think about pretty girls. Or quadratic equations. I'll figure out a plan.
You're just wasting time, Jones. The only option is to fight our way out.
Don't listen to him, Doc. Ju Stay. Calm.
Ooo oo aah!
Do you want to end up in a lab, Bruce? Poked and prodded for the rest of your life?
And who knows what they'll do to Jones and Monkey!
AARGH!

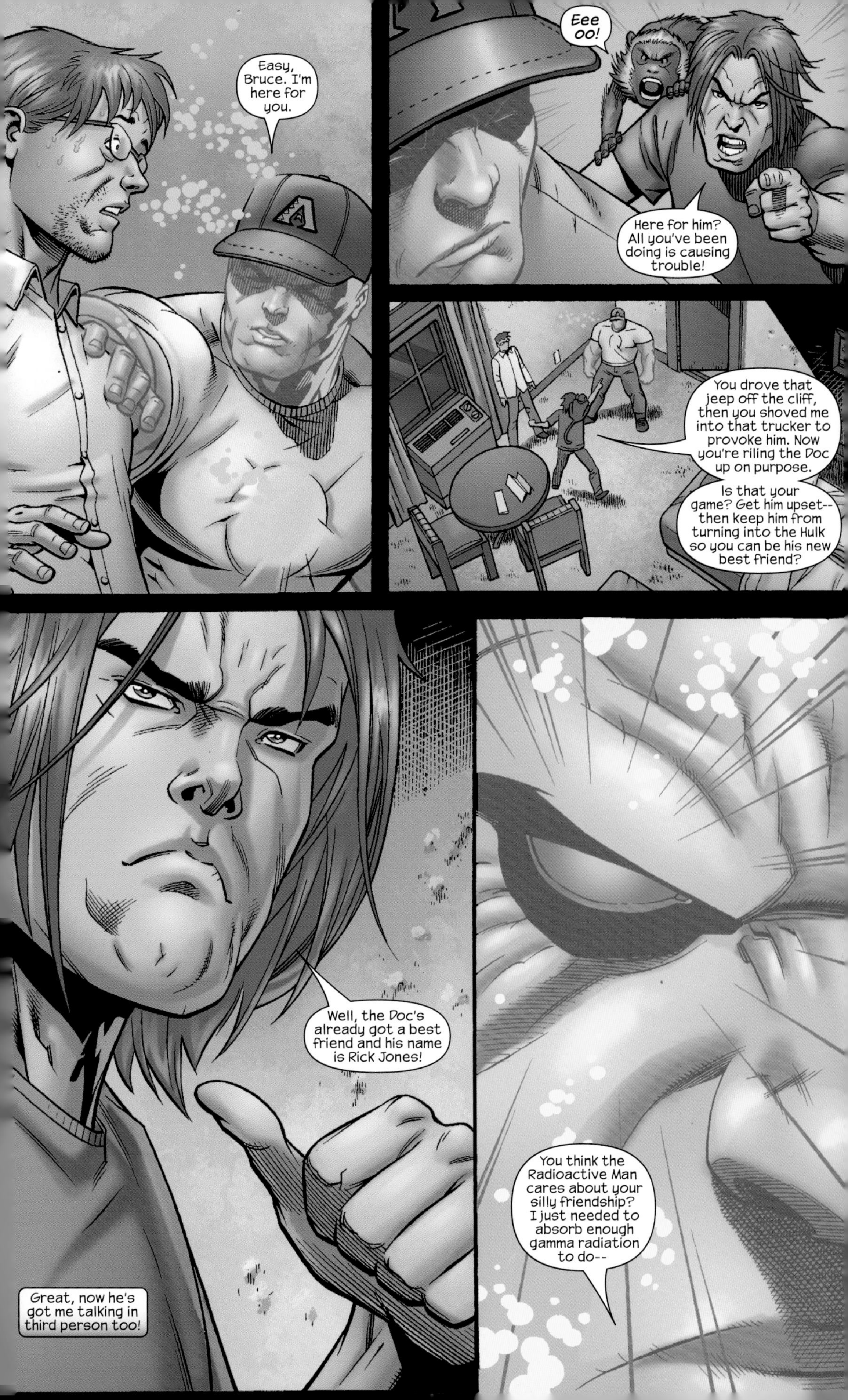
Easy, Bruce. I'm here for you.
Eee oo!
Here for him? All you've been doing is causing trouble!
You drove that jeep off the cliff, then you shoved me into that trucker to provoke him. Now you're riling the Doc up on purpose.
Is that your game? Get him upset--then keep him from turning into the Hulk so you can be his new best friend?
Well, the Doc's already got a best friend and his name is Rick Jones!
Great, now he's got me talking in third person too!
You think the Radioactive Man cares about your silly friendship? I just needed to absorb enough gamma radiation to do--

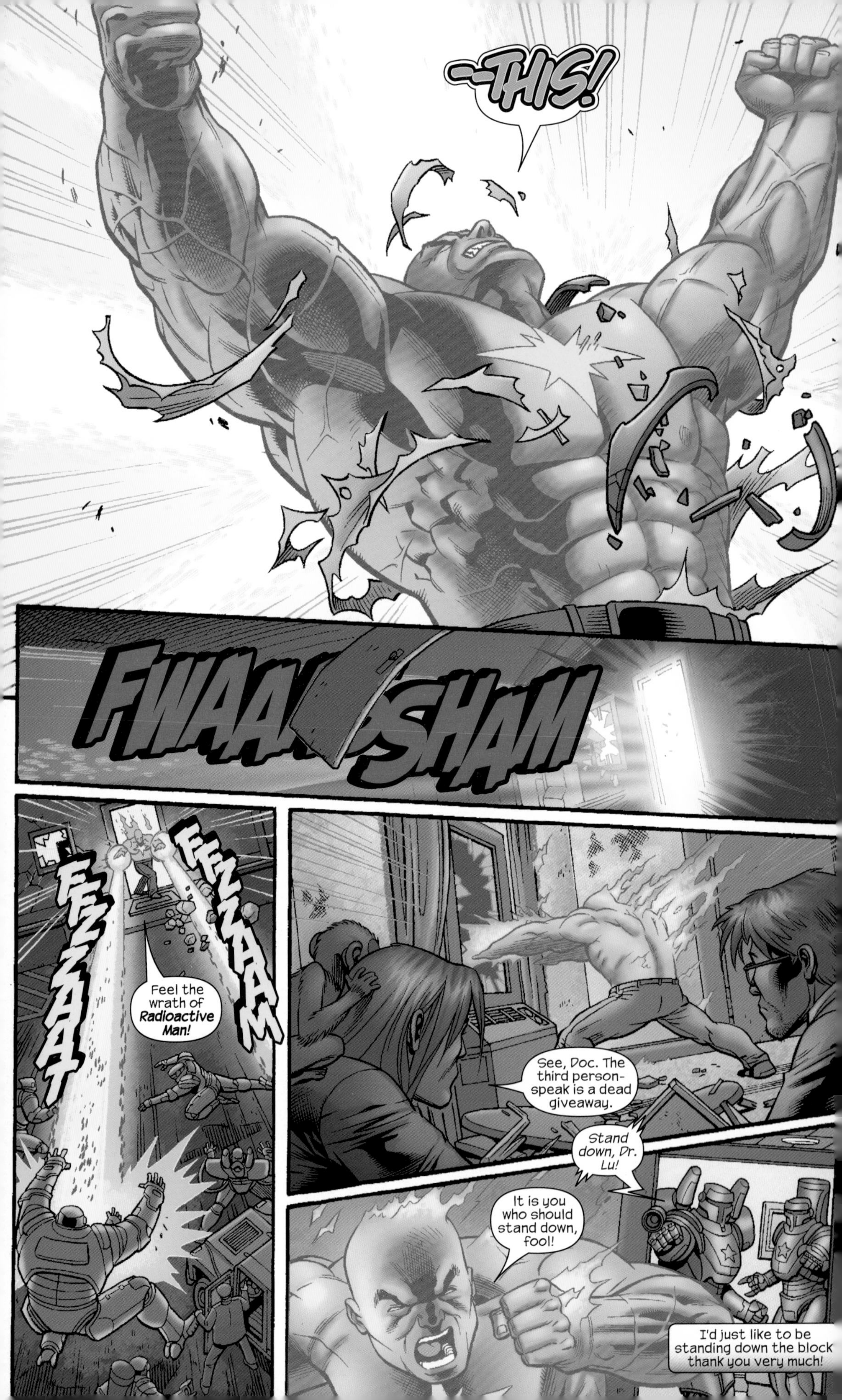
--THIS!
FWAAM SHAM
FFZZAAT
FFZZAAM
Feel the wrath of Radioactive Man!
See, Doc. The third person-speak is a dead giveaway.
Stand down, Dr. Lu!
It is you who should stand down, fool!
I'd just like to be standing down the block thank you very much!

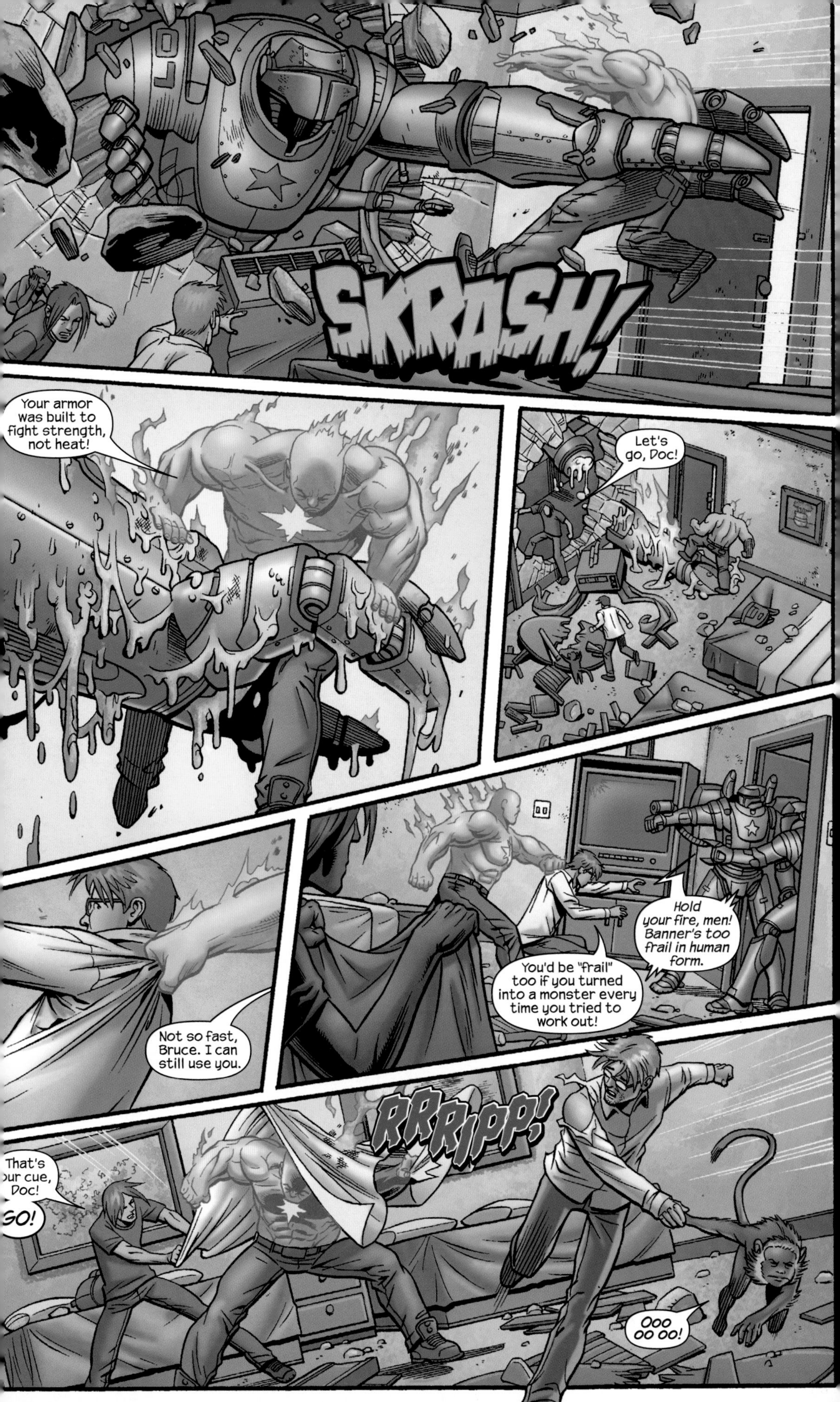
SKRASH!
Your armor was built to fight strength, not heat!
Let's go, Doc!
Hold your fire, men! Banner's too frail in human form.
You'd be "frail" too if you turned into a monster every time you tried to work out!
Not so fast, Bruce. I can still use you.
RRRIPP!
That's our cue, Doc!
GO!
OOO OO OO!

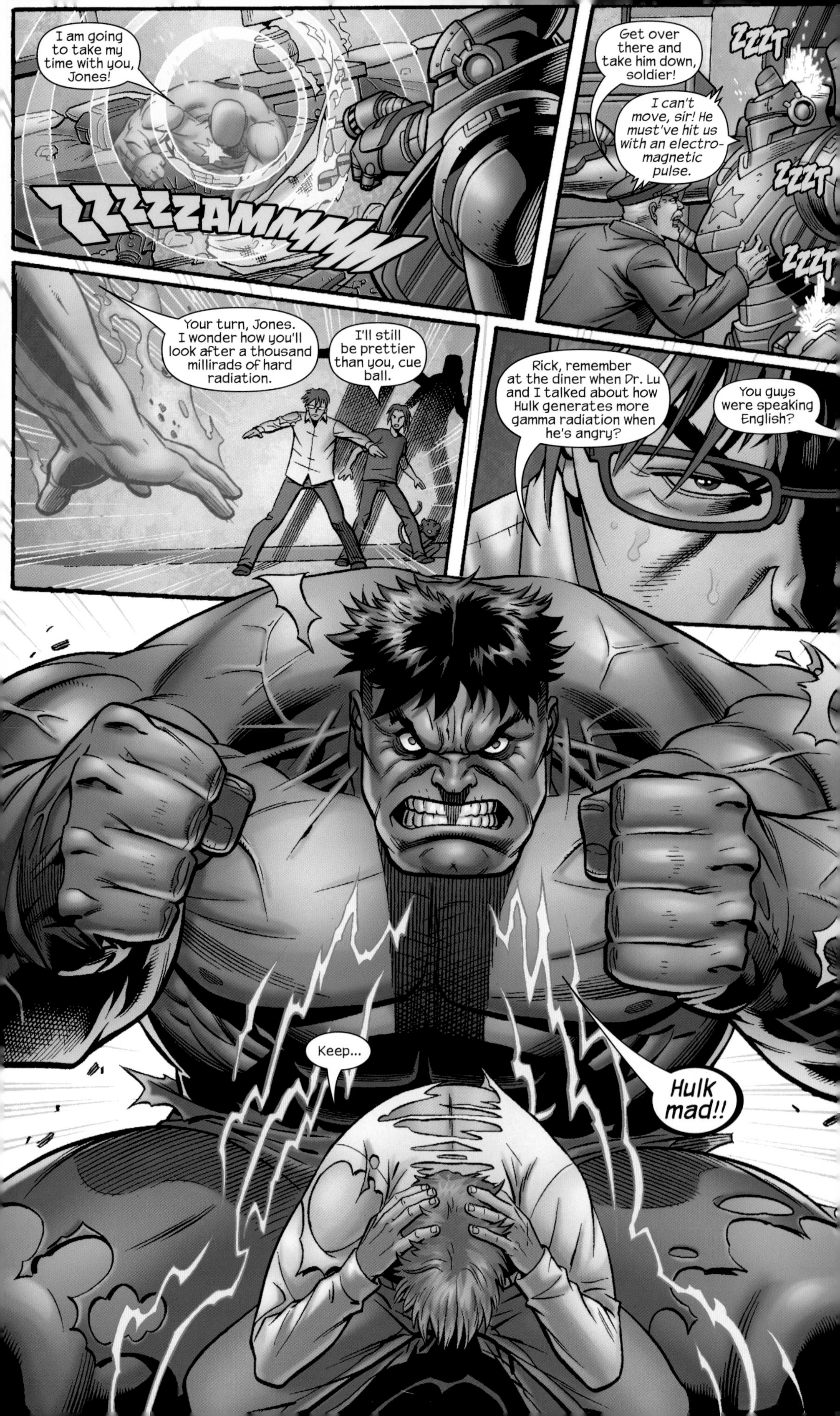
I am going to take my time with you, Jones!
ZZZZZAMMMMM
Get over there and take him down, soldier!
I can't move, sir! He must've hit us with an electro-magnetic pulse.
ZZZT
ZZZT
ZZZT
Your turn, Jones. I wonder how you'll look after a thousand millirads of hard radiation.
I'll still be prettier than you, cue ball.
Rick, remember at the diner when Dr. Lu and I talked about how Hulk generates more gamma radiation when he's angry?
You guys were speaking English?
Keep...
Hulk mad!!

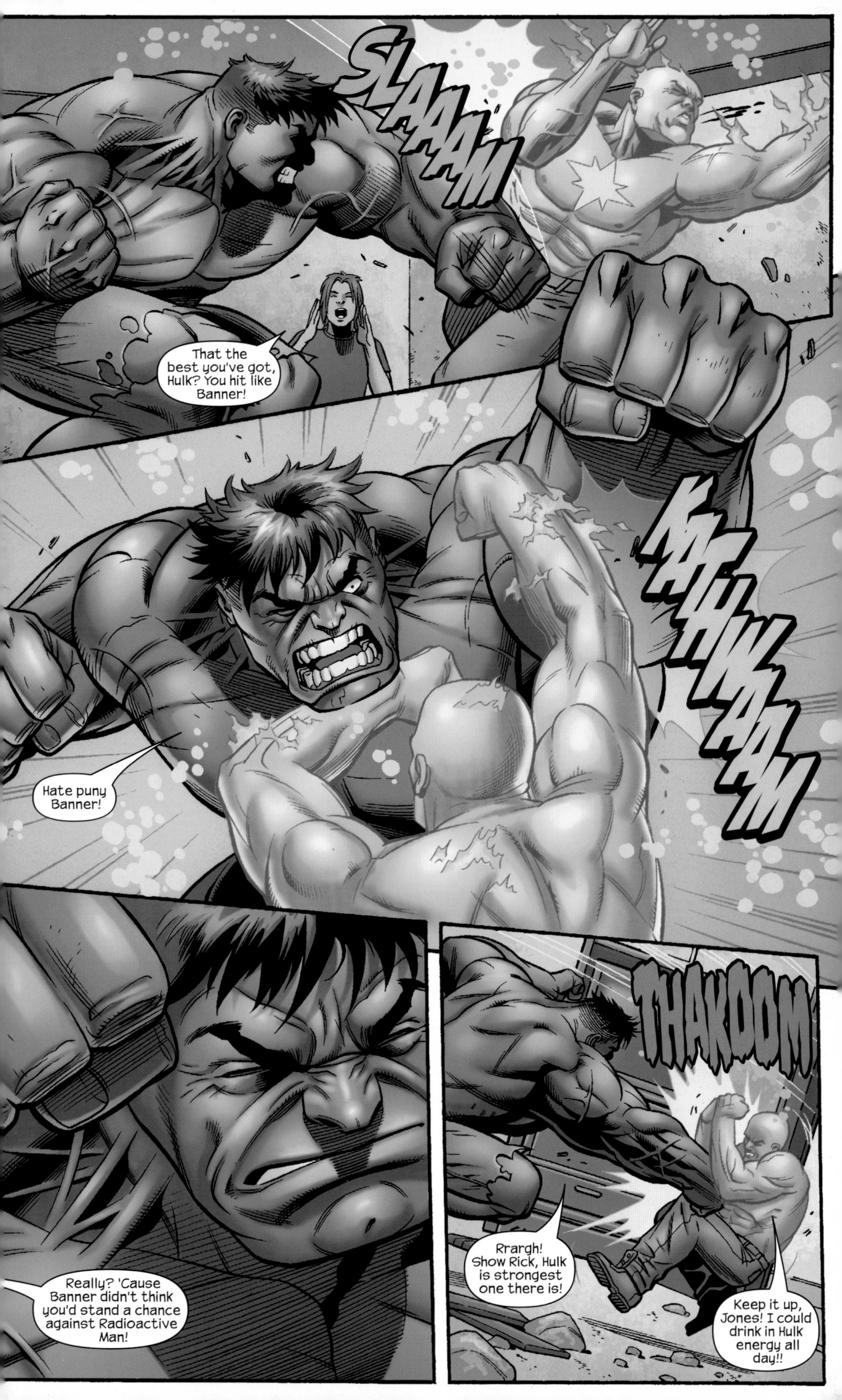
SLAAAAM
That the best you've got, Hulk? You hit like Banner!
KATHWAAAM
Hate puny Banner!
THAKOOM
Really? 'Cause Banner didn't think you'd stand a chance against Radioactive Man!
Rrargh! Show Rick, Hulk is strongest one there is!
Keep it up, Jones! I could drink in Hulk energy all day!!

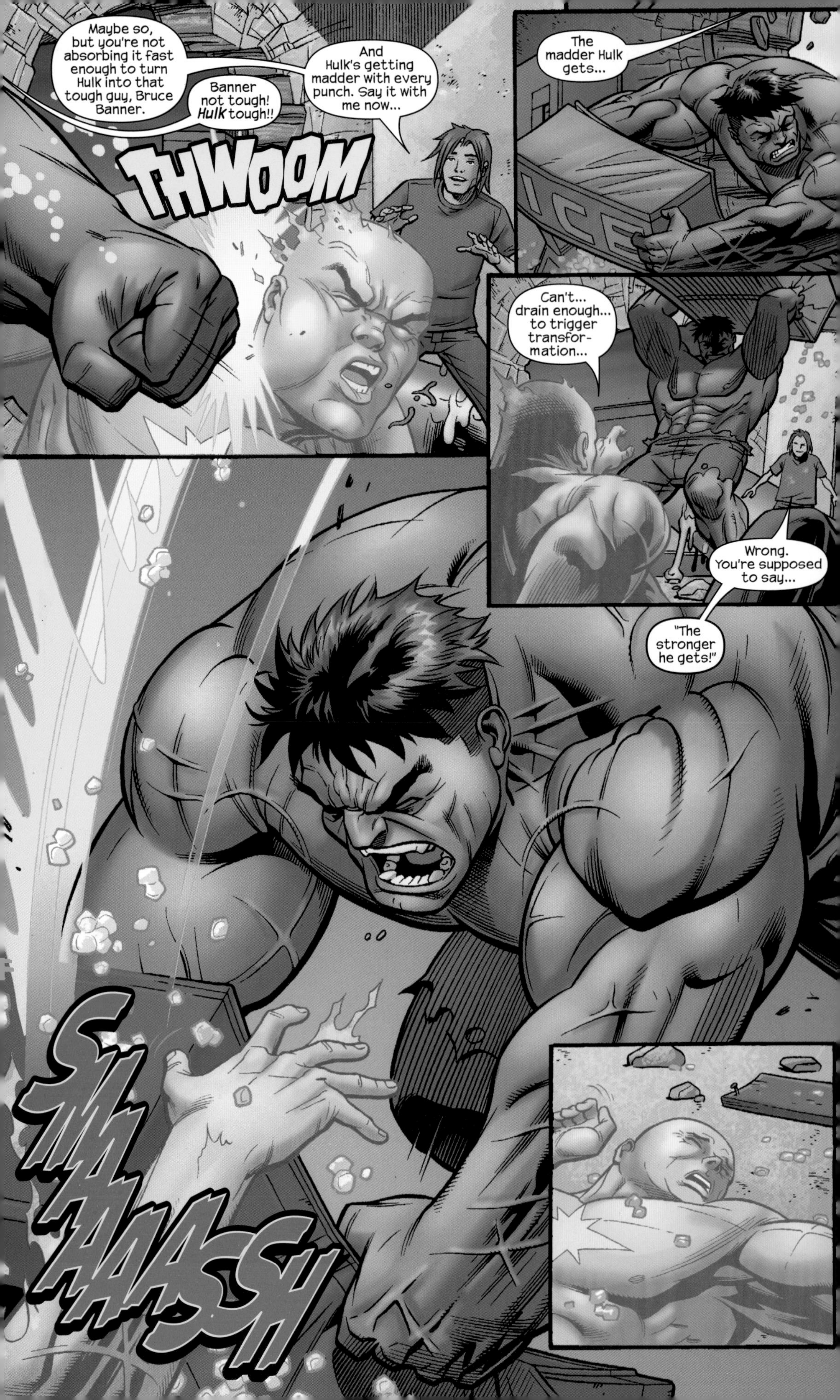

Maybe so, but you're not absorbing it fast enough to turn Hulk into that tough guy, Bruce Banner.
Banner not tough! *Hulk* tough!!
And Hulk's getting madder with every punch. Say it with me now...
THWOOM
The madder Hulk gets...
Can't... drain enough... to trigger transfor-mation...
Wrong. You're supposed to say...
"The stronger he gets!"
SHHHASSH

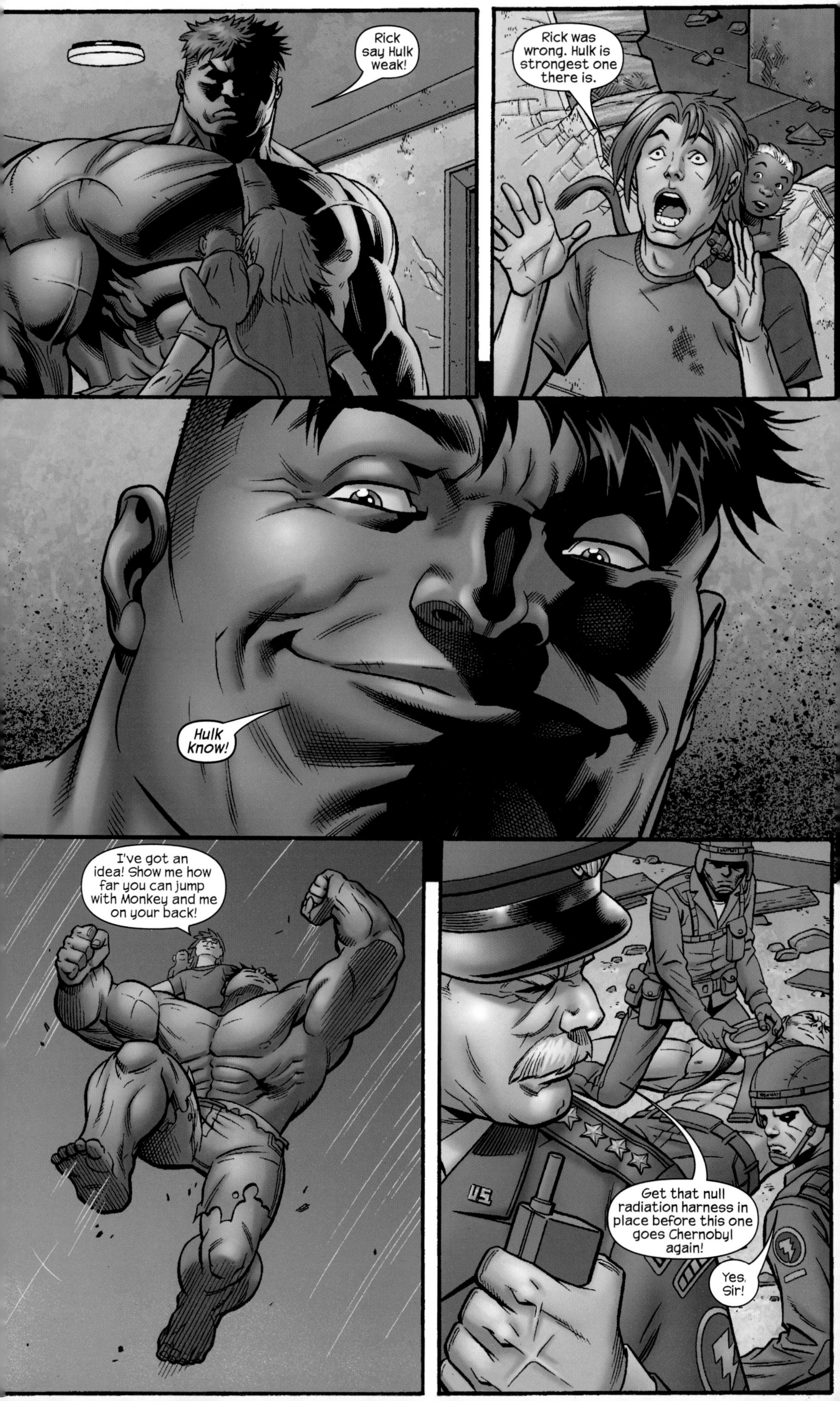
Rick say Hulk weak!
Rick was wrong. Hulk is strongest one there is.
Hulk know!
I've got an idea! Show me how far you can jump with Monkey and me on your back!
Get that null radiation harness in place before this one goes Chernobyl again!
Yes, Sir!

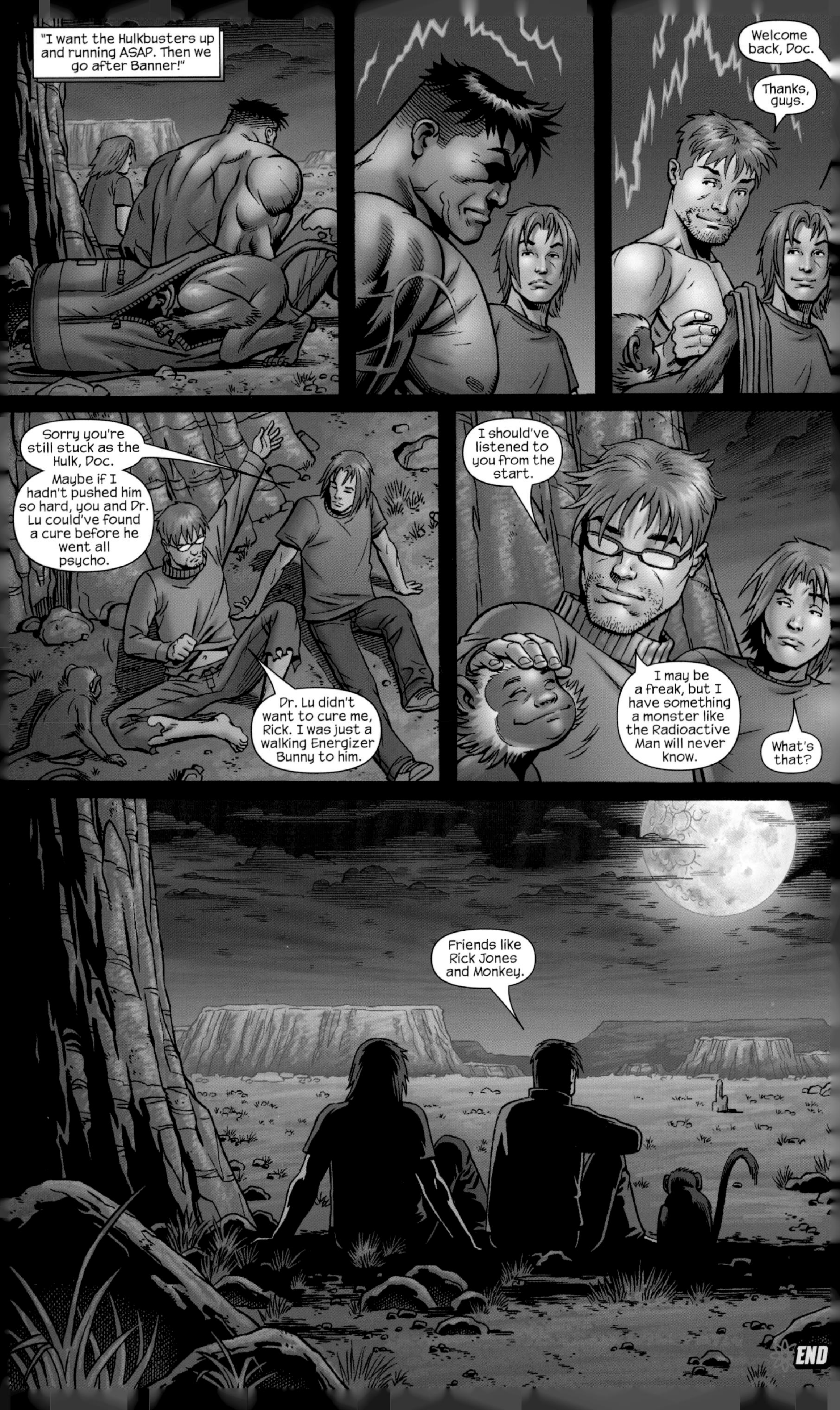
"I want the Hulkbusters up and running ASAP. Then we go after Banner!"
Welcome back, Doc.
Thanks, guys.
Sorry you're still stuck as the Hulk, Doc.
Maybe if I hadn't pushed him so hard, you and Dr. Lu could've found a cure before he went all psycho.
Dr. Lu didn't want to cure me, Rick. I was just a walking Energizer Bunny to him.
I should've listened to you from the start.
I may be a freak, but I have something a monster like the Radioactive Man will never know.
What's that?
Friends like Rick Jones and Monkey.
END

DANIELLE STEEL

Najpopularniejsza dziś na świecie pisarka, niekwestionowana gwiazda literatury kobiecej, piękna, utalentowana i pracowita, oczarowała rzesze czytelniczek na wszystkich kontynentach. Opublikowała już 60 książek, których łączny nakład osiągnął rekordową liczbę 529 milionów egzemplarzy, a każda nowa trafia nieodmiennie na czołowe miejsca najpoważniejszych list bestsellerów. Od piętnastu lat Danielle Steel zachwyca swą twórczością również Polki, przebojem zdobywszy nasz rynek czytelniczy. Na czym polega tajemnica jej sukcesu? Bez wątpienia na tym, że świat jej powieści jest światem rzeczywistym, a problemy osób w nich występujących — autentyczne. Wszak pomysły, jak sama powiada, czerpie z życia. A jej życie nie było — co pewnie niektórych zaskoczy — usłane różami; zaznała nie tylko szczęścia i radości, lecz również goryczy niepowodzeń i zawodów miłosnych, bólu rozstania, rozpaczy po utracie dorastającego syna... Jednakże od 30 lat na kartach swych powieści niezmiennie daje wyraz przeświadczeniu, iż dobrem można przezwyciężyć zło, a nienawiść miłością, naprawić wyrządzoną krzywdę, wykorzystać jedyną szansę. Każda czytelniczka w bohaterkach jej książek znajdzie trochę z Danielle Steel i zarazem trochę z... siebie. Dlatego tak trudno nam o nich zapomnieć i wciąż czekamy na nowe.

Nakładem Wydawnictwa „Książnica"
ukazały się powieści

CHATA • DŁUGA DROGA DO DOMU
DOM THURSTONÓW • DUCH
JAK GROM Z NIEBA • KALEJDOSKOP
KOCHANIE • KONIEC LATA
MIŁOŚĆ SILNIEJSZA NIŻ ŚMIERĆ • OKUP • PIERŚCIONKI
PIĘĆ DNI W PARYŻU
PRZEPRAWY • RADOŚĆ PRZEZ ŁZY
RANDKI W CIEMNO • RAZ W ŻYCIU
RYTM SERCA • SAMOTNY ORZEŁ
SEKRETY • ŚLUB
ŚWIATŁO MOICH OCZU • TERAZ I NA ZAWSZE
W SIECI • WSZYSTKO CO NAJLEPSZE
ZUPEŁNIE OBCY CZŁOWIEK • ZWIASTUN MIŁOŚCI

Książnica

Dla Billa, Beatrix i Nicholasa
w dowód najgłębszej miłości

Dla Phyllis Westberg
z wyrazami przywiązania i wdzięczności